For all the birds in the garden - M

For Stuart and Richard - D

BLOOMSBURY
CHILDREN'S
BOOKS

First published in Great Britain in 2004 by Bloomsbury Publishing Plc
38 Soho Square, London, W1D 3HB

Text copyright © Dosh Archer 2004
Illustrations copyright © Dosh and Mike Archer 2004
The moral rights of Dosh Archer and Mike Archer to be identified as
the authors and illustrators have been asserted

A CIP catalogue record of this book is available from the British Library

ISBN 0 7475 6463 9

Printed in Hong Kong by South China Printing Co

10 9 8 7 6 5 4 3 2 1

Yellow Bird, Black Spider

Dosh and Mike Archer

BLOOMSBURY
CHILDREN'S
BOOKS

Yellow Bird,
blue boat

'Why don't you fly across the sea?' asked Black Spider.

'I like to sail, actually,'
said Yellow Bird.

Yellow Bird,
white hotel

'Why don't you
make a lovely, cosy nest?'
asked Black Spider.

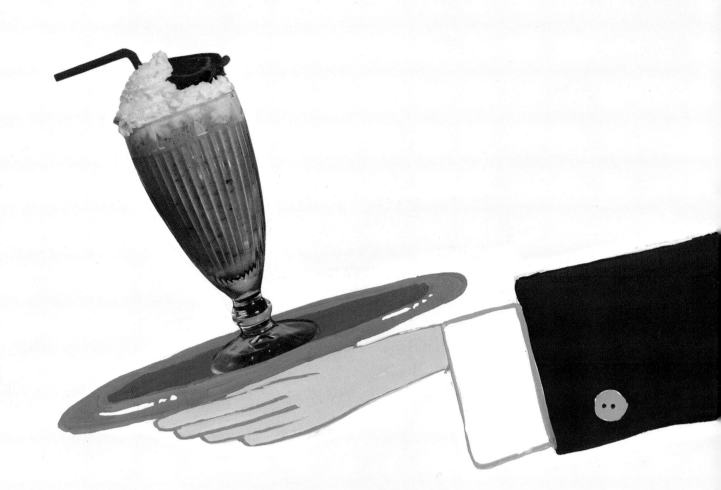

'I like hotels, actually,' said Yellow Bird.

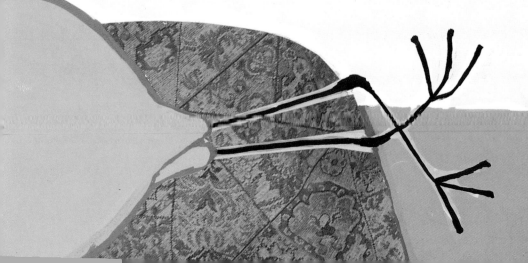

Yellow Bird,
red guitar

'Why don't you
sing *tweet, tweet, tweet,*
in a beautiful way?'
asked Black Spider.

*'I like to strum, actually,'
said Yellow Bird.*

'I like dancing on the beach,
the feel of sand on my toes . . .

I like peace and quiet, vanilla ice-cream,

having baths, and wearing stripy socks.'

'Birds don't usually
wear stripy socks,'
said Black Spider.

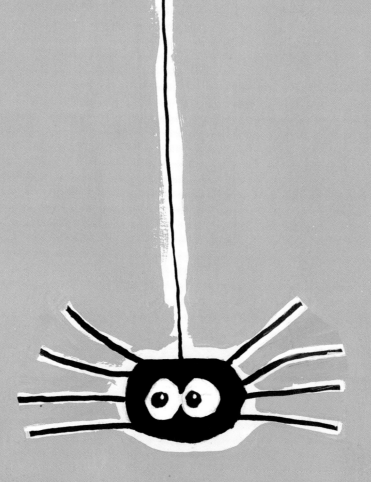

Yellow Bird,
Black Spider

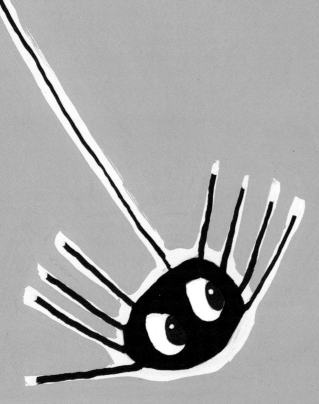

'Why don't you eat
some yummy, squelchy worms?'
asked Black Spider.

'Actually,' said Yellow Bird,

'I like to eat spiders.'